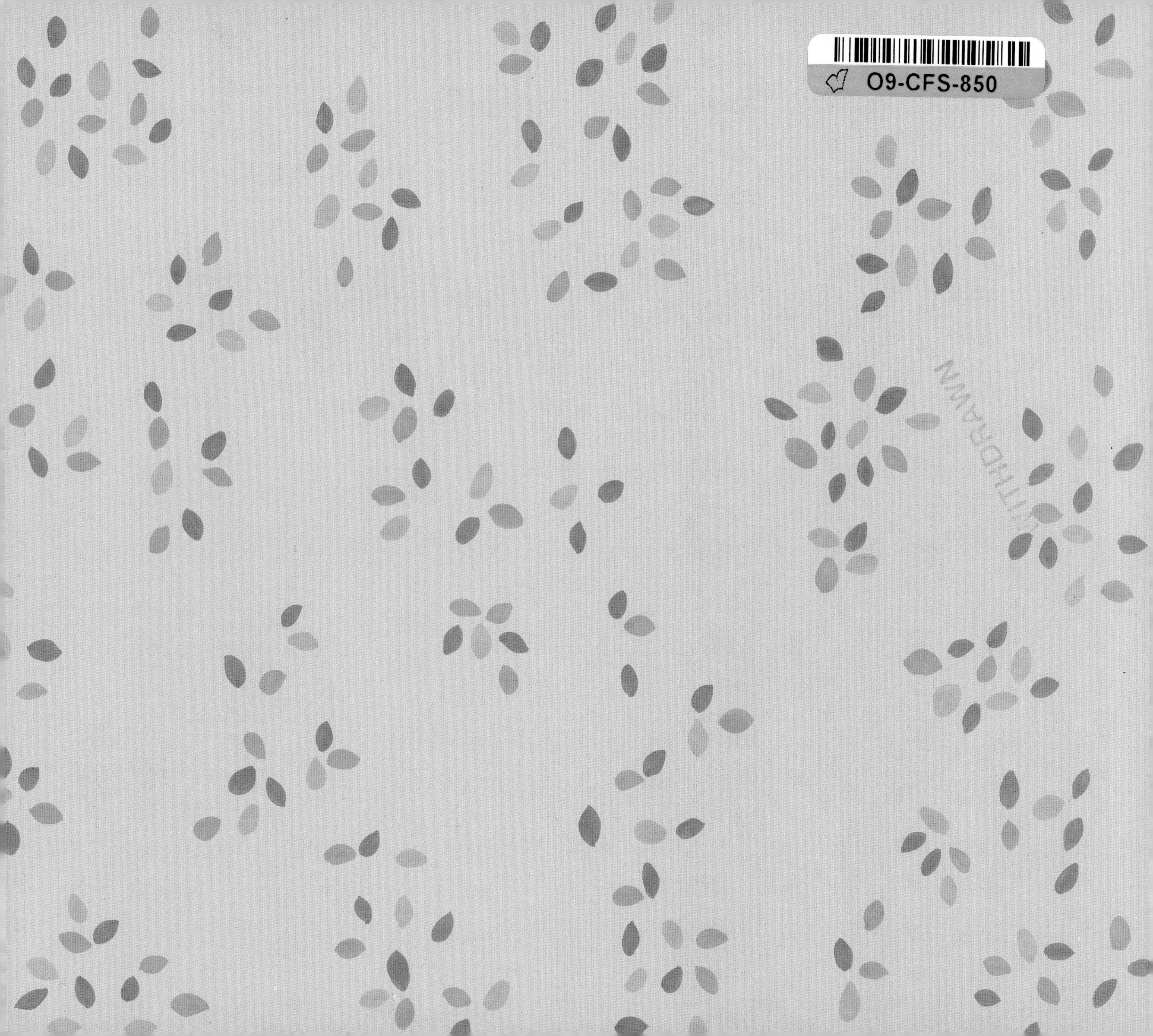

A name is a sound that follows you around.

Visit us on the Web! rhcbooks.com

Educators and librarians, for a variety of teaching tools, visit us at RHTeachersLibrarians.com

Library of Congress Cataloging-in-Publication Data is available upon request.
ISBN 978-1-5247-1419-2 (trade) — ISBN 978-1-5247-1420-8 (lib. bdg.) — ISBN 978-1-5247-1421-5 (ebook)

MANUFACTURED IN CHINA
10 9 8 7 6 5 4 3 2 1
First Edition

A NAME FOR BABY

LIZI BOYD

Random House New York

Baby was born tiny, pink and furless.

"You're a beauty," cooed Mother Mouse.

Baby blinked.

The field mice came and gazed at her.
"What will you name her?"

"A name has to hum.
I'll listen for one," said Mother.

Mother Mouse set a table with nibbles,
nuts and soup. Everyone came, one by one.

Mimi Meadowlark sang a spring song.
Baby listened.
“Meadow Mouse?” Mother wondered.
“A nice name, but that’s not it.”

Blake Snake brought a little moth.

Baby watched it circling round.

“Moth Mouse?” Mother wondered.

“No, that doesn’t fit.”

Lolly Ladybug brought a maidenhair fern.
She tickled Baby's toes.

"Maiden Mouse?" Mother wondered.
"A fairy-tale name, but not for Baby."

Sadie Snail brought a blanket of moss.
Baby patted it and squeaked.

“Mossy Mouse?” Mother wondered.
“A soft, quiet sound, but not the one.”

Kiki Cat came, twirling her tail.
“When you’re bigger, Baby, maybe we’ll play,”
she purred. “What’s your name anyway?”

“A name is a sound that follows you around.
I’m listening for one,” said Mother.

“Greenie Grasshopper and Merle Squirrel are late,” said the field mice.

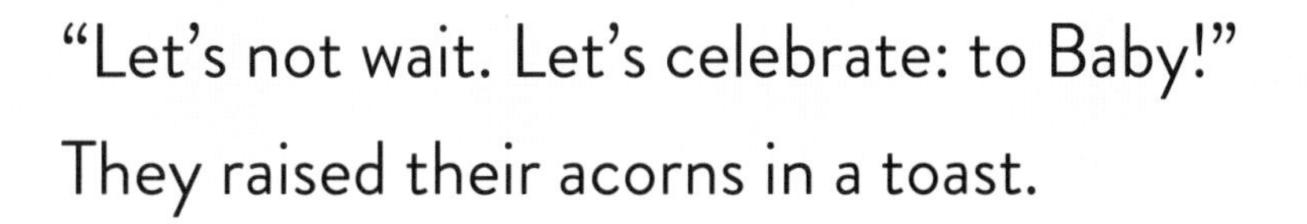

"Let's not wait. Let's celebrate: to Baby!"

They raised their acorns in a toast.

Greenie Grasshopper came just in time.
He brought mayflowers.
Baby wiggled her nose and smiled.

"May Mouse?" Mother wondered.

"Baby likes it. May—it's sweet but too short."

And with the night came Moon.

“Baby’s a beauty. What’s her name?”

“I’m listening for one,” said Mother.

"The night sky is quiet. I'll listen too,"
said Moon as he climbed higher.

“Moon Mouse?” Mother wondered.

“It has a hum, just not enough of one.”

Merle Squirrel came, carrying a stem of milkweed pods.
Everyone blew the silky wisps into the sky.
“Did you wish for a name?” asked Merle Squirrel.
“A wish is a secret until it comes true.
I have a wish, but I’m listening too,” said Mother.

"I hear *Moon* and *flower* and *may*. If I put them together like this—May Moonflower Mouse—it's your name!"

"A very big name. A name I can't say," said Sadie Snail.

"May Moonflower Mouse needs a nickname too," chattered the field mice. "A name we can call. And a name we can sing!"

“Then she’ll be May May to family and friends,”
said Mother.
Everyone blew May May wishes and kisses.

May May squeaked and smiled.

In the quiet sky Moon heard his friends calling, "May May." And his friends saw Moon's faint smile, appearing and disappearing, as he went rolling by.

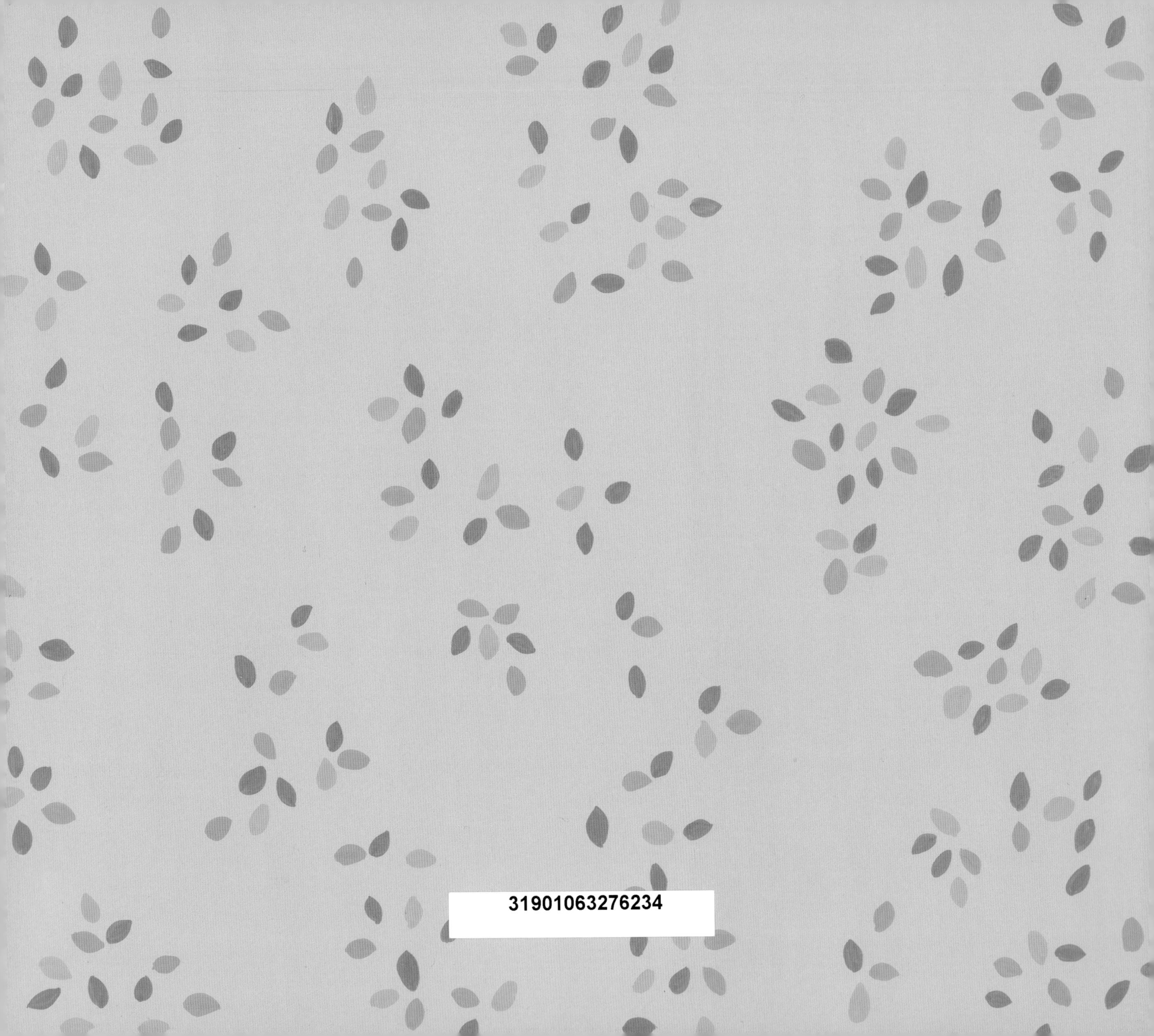